Redeemer's Song
THE TRIUMPH OF MERCY

J NADA

Redeemer's Song, The Triumph Of Mercy

Copyright 2012 – 2014, Mercy Media, LLC

Notes on grammar:

For the most part, formal rules of punctuation have not been followed. Since much of the text is metered verse, punctuation is kept to a minimum and is used only for readability and for grouping of related phrases.

Characteristics of God are capitalized, because the nature and character of God are synonymous with His person.

Proper names relating to satan and his angels are lower case, except at the beginning of a line or in a heading

Published by Mercy Media, LLC
http://www.mercy-media.com

Mercy Media ™

ISBN: 978-0-9911616-0-7

Dedication

To our brothers and sisters who, while in prison, are learning to live as free men and women.

To those who were born into difficult life situations – who were born in the bottom of the ninth, down by 10 runs, with two outs, two strikes and a broken bat – but whose lives are a demonstration of the power of redemption.

To those who show us that, no matter how deep the hole, God's love is deeper still.

To those who teach us to live each day dependent on God's grace.

To those who are choosing a better path.

For I know the thoughts that I think toward you, saith the LORD, thoughts of peace, and not of evil, to give you an expected end. Then shall ye call upon me, and ye shall go and pray unto me, and I will hearken unto you. And ye shall seek me, and find [me], when ye shall search for me with all your heart. And I will be found of you, saith the LORD: and I will turn away your captivity, and I will gather you from all the nations, and from all the places whither I have driven you, saith the LORD; and I will bring you again into the place whence I caused you to be carried away captive. [Jeremiah 29:11-14 KJV]

About This Book

Most of this book is written like a song, so the lines follow a definite meter and are grouped loosely into verses. The sections that are in song form are written in common meter, with four "beats" per line (in musical terms, the "beat" is in common time) – like many ballads, folksongs and hymns. For example:

"Amazing Grace" (1779) –

With many older songs, words were first written as metered verse (often common meter) and were not set to a particular melody. People would then take the words and sing them to popular tunes of the day.

The text of "Amazing Grace" has, over its history, been associated with more than 20 different tunes. It was not until 1835 that "Amazing Grace" was first associated with the tune "New Britain," the tune that is typically thought of as "Amazing Grace" today.

If you read the words of "Amazing Grace" out loud, you will hear a "beat" in those words that is similar to the meter of this book.

Hope you enjoy it.

Redeemer's Song
THE TRIUMPH OF MERCY

Prologue

The Son of God
The Son of Man
Hung bleeding, bruised
Against the sky

A fragile case, that for short while
Had held the Lord in human form.
That fragile case now broken, crushed
Abused until it lost its hold
Eternal Life, once housed within
Would soon escape Its mortal form.

And there He hung 'tween dust and sky
The Holy One now made our sin.
With dying breath, but voice still strong
The Lion roared that all was done.

His voice of triumph, through the realms
Resounded clear, so all would know
Redemption's plan was fully worked
The battle won, the Victor sure.

The horror of this final day
When Love was tortured by Its own
There clearly showed the cost to pay
The depths of guilt, the ransom price.
The Love of God on clear display
How large a price that He must bear
To bring an end to death's domain
And banish darkness to its cell.

To understand this fearful scene
To see the players and the cause
Look back before the dawn of time
Eternal Love sat on the throne.

PART 1.

BEFORE THE EARTH

Chapter 1.
Love's Prelude

A. The Realm Of Love

Long before the age of man
Before the earth was given form
A perfect Heart sat on the throne
And Life came forth with every breath.
Eternal Power joined with Love
And Love the greatest of commands.
Eternal Goodness wrapped in might
The universe, as one, at rest.

Almighty God, with endless Life
Outside the bounds of space and time
The Lord Of All, the Perfect One
Eternity without an end.

From deep within that purest Light
Without a spot or darkened hue
His Glory pulsed and bathed the worlds
His Spirit freely flowed to all.
From deep within that perfect Love
Without a shadow, flaw or shade
Flowed Life Eternal, peace and joy
And all creation joined as one.

A timeless music calmly rose
Throughout creation's vast expanse --
Each stream and sea, with swell and calm
Created joyful harmony.
Each galaxy, with countless stars
Reverberated melody.
Each distant mountain, standing tall
With anthem, gave its voice to song.

A host of beings filled the realm
With soul and will unique to each.
Created ones of noble state
Their love for God flowed with each breath.
The universe was their domain
And yet regardless of the span
Each one beheld with clearest sight
The Glory of the Perfect One.

In unity they lived and worked
Not knowing toil or sweat or pain.

And in the realm where Glory ruled
From every blade and rock and branch
A song of praise forever rose
In undirected harmonies.
The praise of God forever swelled
Not forced, coerced, but from the soul
With each created heart and mind
As one, a symphony of praise.

B. Love Can Be Hard To See

To us who live an earthly life
This reign of Love seems truly strange --
The stuff of legend, cast in dreams
A children's tale, an infant's wish
The inner cry from broken hearts
A gasp for hope and small relief.

In truth, it is our earthly lives
That make up little more than dream
A single breath, a hurried sigh
Then what we hold will slip away.
This journey short, in human skin
This fog, this mist dropped on our eyes
Can keep True Love from coming in
And hide our sight from what is real.

But still, the realm where Love is King
Does sure exist and always has --
Not written in our intellect
Not birthed from weak philosophy.
For through the years the earth has marched
As men and women penned their thoughts
No one surmised and no one guessed
That --
God is Love.

How could our knowledge fall so short?
We thought God cold, cruel and aloof.
We saw Him manufacture woe
And judged Him as the source of pain
An ear closed to our suffering
Indifferent silence to our cry.

Our hist'ry as the human race
Is proof enough of simple truth --
That broken lives produced our hurt
And our own hands forged every tear.
For once a people turn from Love
Our souls become a home for pain.

C. Redemption Helps Us See

Yet, as Redemption's work is seen
The true effect is there revealed
For Light and Good, Redeeming Love
Are rooted in the heart of God.
While death and woe and all its pain
Are only safe where darkness dwells.

Against this curtain of our lives
Against the culture we designed
Redemption helps us understand
That God is not like us at all.
For when we see the heart of God
And understand the price He paid
We start to see Eternal Love --
A Mercy strong, with Justice pure.

Chapter 2.
The Birth of Sin

To understand Redemption's price
To know the depth of boundless Love
To understand the course of sin
We take a look at those who turned.

A. The First Rebellion

Pride crept in and built a home
In one so fair, one near the throne.
Archangel of the highest rank
Whose place was next to Heaven's heart.

As worship swelled and filled the air
This angel, Lucifer by name
Began to cast an inward gaze
And turn his thoughts away from God.
Why was his station lower than
Eternal Glory on the throne?

The thought of "I" – exalted self
Lodged in his soul, and pride was born.
Into this world where all was right
A single stain began to form.

This subtle seed had burrowed deep
And there it found a fertile place --
To nourish self, to spread its roots
To search for life on which to feed
To stay there hidden, for a time
To find a place, so it could grow.

This haughty seed began to sprout --
First shoot, then blade, so small, so pale
So frail at first, but as it spread
A bud emerged and birthed its fruit
The fruit matured, came forth as sin.

Now sin was born in secret place --
Each day it grew, took shape and form
It stretched its arms away from God
Away from all that made for good.
Embraced itself, its own desires
To lift itself to higher place
To take its stand defiantly
Against the rule of Love.

As pride took root and stoutly grew
A new design lodged in the mind
"I will arise and be like God
My throne will be above the Lord's."
From inward gaze, to need for more
Ambition was the driving force
"I too deserve my own acclaim
For glory also flows through me."

Pride's discontent to walk with Love
Pride's own desires preeminent
It would not bow, it could not serve
But strove to gain a higher place.

So in that one who was so fair
A dimness crept, as Light repelled
And in that place, where beauty shone
The features bend, contort, deform.

The time was right to make a move
This angel fair, with heart aflame
With followers, in army formed
Rose up to conquer Heaven's King.
Assault was made, the battle swift
But they no match for Heaven's power
For pride will work to make you blind
And lift you up before the fall.

Still on they fought, though half in size
They thought their passion gave them strength
Their revolution quickly failed
The universe, no place to hide.
In chains, they marched before the Judge
Then quickly dropped into abyss.

B. The Abyss

1. Darkness' Home

Cast out they were, to unlit place
Where Light and dark could not embrace
Rebellion cast out to this realm
A chasm deep of dim-lit night.
A foul, dark stench, not pierced by stars
A place that pride could call its own
And, by cruel reign, enforce its will.

They would be masters of their fate
And so it was that they performed
Their plans and traps with clumsy art
And won them this eternal hole.
Exalted "I" who sought to be
Adored by all, now brought so low
Dropped in a place far from the Lord.

In deep crevasse, an empty hole
The devil rose to take his place.
So filled with rage, with gnarled heart
He set about to force his will --
To build his throne by cruel design
And press his reign within the pit.

2. Satan's Reign

He looked about to build his world
To see what assets he possessed
He was cut off from Love and Light
Now cut off from the Lord Himself.

There was no Life, here only death.
Without the Light, pure darkness fell.
Where Truth had lived, now only lies.
Creative Faith was turned to fear.
All joyous hope became despair.
Where Grace had ruled, the king now pride.

So in the dusk, as Light repelled
He toiled to build his kingdom hard.
Forged in the gloom with hate and lies
He would be lord of his domain.
On sand corrupt, his throne secure
The lord of lies sat down to rule.

Chaotic scene within the pit --
The fallen ones, who just like him
Had turned from Love to serve the "I"
To follow only self's desires.
With no more sense of right or wrong
This fallen mob must be controlled.
His will and rule would be unchecked
This rabble scum be made to bow.

With hatred cruel, malevolent
He set to order his intent.

3. The Darkangels

His kingdom was controlled in bands.
Three dark battalions in the night.

Destruction first, the strongest one --
Apollyon, as later called
So large in size, with massive claws
To bring down war against all good.
Then hatred, fear and pride arose
Three captains standing by his side
To carry out his word and will
To serve the fallen overlord.

Deception was the next in line --
A shadow mist with shades of grey
With voice in whisper, veiled from sight
A swirling smoke, that none could hold.
Not organized by rank and place
Just swarms of creatures, hunched and vile
Who hid themselves in shadow form
To whisper lies then they were gone.

The final dark one named **desire** --
With belly large and bulbous eyes
Who after feeding, craves again
No rest, no pause from wanting more.
To him, as well, three captains bowed
As greed and lust and envy rise
To take their place beside this beast
To play their part, do his command.

4. *The Demon Caste*

So satan's realm was organized
And freedom banished from the heart
Each angel locked in iron bands
Locked down by fear and lies and pain.
They once were free, now forced to serve --
Captivity without an end.

The fallen ones could scarce recall
How they had lived when they were free
Once free to choose and walk in Love
With freedom, serve the Holy One.
The joy they knew once had no bounds
Now all they felt – tormented pain.
Their only path – to go along.
This tragic role now forced to play
To never see the stars again.

A hope of rest, a simple pause
Is nowhere found
Has fled the realm.

Though foul air pressed, tormented sore
'twas not the place that stirred such pain.
It was the endless gulf within --
A fallen soul, tormented thoughts
A poison stain left there by sin.

These angels, trapped in night and toil
'til nothing good was in their hearts
Each fallen one, more empty still
As evil thoughts boiled deep within.
The weight of what they had become
Had dragged them deeper in abyss.

These fallen ones, who once could see
With clear-eyed gaze, through boundless space
Their vision lost, in dim-lit view
Can barely see a length or two.
Illumination all but gone
Their eyes adapt to little spark
The sickly, greenish glow of pride
Plus scattered fires that fueled on hate.

These tangled souls, once bathed in Light
Whose features shined with noble grace --
Once beautiful, beyond compare
Their faces now an ugly boil
Contorted to reflect the state
Of evil in their fallen souls.

They had been promised higher place
That they would rise, and they would rule
The Light and Glory that they knew
Would someday bow to their control.
They thought to own, to hold for self
The higher ways that made for good
But they had only grasped a lie
Angelic reason warped by pride.

For Love and Light and Life and Good
Do not exist apart from God
For God is Love, and Love is whole
Not something to be clutched or held.
Love only lives when it is shared
Not as a servant of desire
The ego cannot fashion Love
Love misapplied is never there.

5. *Waiting For Revenge*

To keep the tumult in its pen
To hold the chaos by its rein
He shepherded their hate and rage
And kept them focused on revenge.
Without this outward gaze of hate
A civil war would surge within.

Their hatred swelled against the Lord
A pounding hate that only grew.
They blamed Him for their low estate
For it was He who cast them out.
Their blinding rage refused to see
It was their course that brought them low.

For God did not create the dark
Or death or sin or hate or rage.
But all these ills that they endured --
That vulgar offspring of their pride --
Had grown from pitch that fills the heart
When God is taken from the soul.

They must revenge, they must repay
The Lord Of Life must be brought low.
A recompense for what had been
Then they, as promised, rise above.
God must be dragged to lower place
And made to suffer for their fall.

But how to win and how to fight
Against the Lord, Almighty One?
Their weapons puny to compare
Their war against the Lord had failed.

For Heaven's power flowed from Love
And Love will always overcome.
The crafty thoughts and hollow aims
Of wicked hearts will always bow.

So in their rage and twisted minds
Demented hope, of sorts, remained --
Tormented, waiting through the years
To find soft place where they could breach
They held their course, to bide their time
To wait until an opening.

Then they would creep, come from the side
And undetected, sow their lies
To plant their hate, secure their rule
With subtle words, supplant the Lord.
Then they would spew out from their jail
To blot out Light and Life and Good
To bring to naught the rule of Love
And plunge creation into night.

Part 2.
NIGHTFALL

Chapter 3.
The Second Battlefield

A. Heaven's Child

1. *The Earth*

A stunning sphere of blue and green
The earth hung closely to its star.
A tiny speck, so small in size
In scope and breadth, a grain of sand.
There nested in a billion stars
Became the place where God would plant
An infant race, the race of man.

Sufficient for this fragile race
That from earth's dust would find their form
Eternal souls that for short while
Would journey on her outer crust.
Each season followed as before
With rain and snow, with hot then cold
Her seeds would sprout and in their course
Bear fruit and grain as food for life.
Providing means of sustenance
The earth would feed its pilgrim bands.

2. The New Race

Out of that dust, God made the man
And breathed in him the breath of Life.
The kiss of God upon his soul
The Life of God within his frame.
And with first view, as eyes could see
The man beheld the face of God.

Next, the woman from his side
To stand an equal, as a bride
A helper, who would add her strength
Protector for this new-formed man.

Two parts together in a drop
To bear the image of their God.

As evening set, as work was done
The Lord would visit this new pair --
To fellowship, instruct and bless
To teach them how they were to live
To walk in freedom, walk in Love
To worship God, to do His will
To draw from Life and tend the earth
Reflecting God in paradise.

3. *The Dark Plan*

The evil one stood far aside
Observing this new family
With jealous hurt, he could recall
How he had once been close to God.
His angry mind still sought revenge
With no remorse for sunken state
He saw a chance to strike the Lord
To make the earth his new abode.

And how he hated these two souls
Their innocence, their times with God
These two enjoyed what he once had
And brought to mind his former state.

But more than that, he saw the Love
That God showed to this new-formed race
He vowed to break the bond they shared
Use people to inflict the blow.
Authority on earth was theirs
So he would take that for his own
To grow his kingdom on this soil
And make advance against the Lord.

For God had blessed with everything
And all was subject to their hand.
The only act they could not do
Was eat of the forbidden fruit.
This simple law, to teach them well
Was more than just a boundary
For all will need to understand
That love includes obedience.

The Lord's command was stated clear
No question as to the result
"For in the day you eat of it
You step onto the path of death."
A death not just of earthly flesh
An end-result much worse than that --
A death that cuts us off from Life
And separates our souls from God.

One certain fruit they could not eat
That fruit of knowledge of the mind
Imperfect sense of good and bad
Creating standards on its own.
For Heaven is the source of Light
A Light not birthed within our minds
God's wisdom shows the proper way
Through Him, we learn both right and wrong.

On this command and consequence
The devil built his strategy --
Deceive this pair to disobey
To walk the path of their own way
To act against the Lord's command
And lock their race in chains of death.

Deception was his only tool
But that enough for his intent
He came with doubt and then desire
He vowed to turn their hearts away.
He would attack the simple rule
That single law of their restraint
He would implant the seed of doubt
To turn them from the Lord's command.

4. *The Big Lie*

The devil wrapped in serpent's skin
With subtle beauty to beguile
He set about to draw these two
And turn their love away from God.

"Oh, has God said?" – the serpent hissed
As pride's foul seed searched for new ground --
To burrow into this new line
To pull their reach away from God.

First, questions posed to foster doubt
And stir up insecurities --
To set the heart to inward gaze
To turn their lives toward selfish end
To brew a false humility
Exalt the mind and nurture pride
To question God's intent and Love
To raise their will against the Lord.

"If God were such a loving One,"
The devil's seed was softly sown,
"He would not hold back anything
Or force you to depend on Him.
He would not keep you in the dark
Or strap you down in innocence."

"All you need, one tiny bite
And knowledge will wash through your minds
Then you can know both right and wrong
With open eyes, judge for yourselves.
You should ascend, be like a god
And show yourself as more than this.
With this new knowledge, lift your state
Become the captains of your fate."

5. The Fall

So as the woman gazed upon
Desire was birthed within her heart
The accusation, whispered soft
Had now become her single thought.
"Well. Hath God said? So where's the harm?"
The woman mused within her thoughts.
"With this new knowledge in our minds
We can arise, judge for ourselves
Determine what is right and wrong
Be masters of a brave, new world."

Her thoughts had joined to single act
A simple taste to find out more
And so she took and ate the fruit
And gave a morsel to the man.

The man stood silent, next to her
He did not speak or contradict
Stood passive to the ways of God
He could have stopped this, but did not.

And so the two took from the tree
And there transgressed the Lord's command
And sealed the fate of all their race
And doomed us to the march of death.

B. The Fallen Realm

1. After The Fall

With single act, the deed was done, and darkness crept into the world – a cold mist, faceless and merciless. Emptiness not perceived by sight, but felt within the depths of soul. An unseen shift, but heart and mind sensed the birth of this new stain. Where Light and Life had blessed the soul, loss and turmoil took their place. With this single act of defiance, the human race started its life-long march into the grave.

Pride, that rebellion against God, against all that is Love, had been planted into the soil of God's new race. Innocence was covered in night, beauty wrapped in fear and doubt, clothes of Glory exchanged for knowledge without God, Love and Life traded for a false sense of independence and control.

The realm of the Spirit – reality – was ripped from the physical world – the habitation of mist.

As sin's curse settled on the once-blessed land, a scene of horror played out in the demon realm. The gates of the abyss were unchained, and its bowels gushed forth in a chaotic surge of evil. With screams and shrieks, they howled and barked, announcing their victory and release. The ancient war had been won by the Almighty, but today was theirs. God's precious world had become their fortress, a beachhead in the endless war. They would have their revenge.

Out they came, in loosely organized groups, each marching behind its own banner. The banners were dark and stiff and each contained a descriptive term -- like "lust," "greed," "pride," "self-righteousness," "gossip," "murder," "oppression" -- to identify the specialty and purpose of the group that followed. On the sticks that held these banners, a jagged writing could be seen where blasphemes and accusations against the Almighty had been crudely carved into the poles. Hell's army marched to secure its new territory.

The angels of God took silent watch at the edge of earth's atmosphere.

Satan slithered toward the Lord, with casual pace, but eyes on alert. He and his group did not fully understand what had happened, but they felt that, somehow, things were different. He sensed an advantage and pressed to see the extent of his boundaries.

"The earth is mine," satan hissed, keeping safely at a distance.

"No, the earth and its glory are still Mine," the Lord replied.

"But Lord," his voice shrill, with all the disdain he would dare, "if I may, I will quote from Your own law, 'The soul that sins must die,'" -- his voice a slimy mixture of pain and mocking. For, in the space that once held his heart, the pain of his own judgment and exile remained, undimmed by the passing of time.

"How ironic," he thought, "the very words that sealed my fate have become my instrument of revenge."

"So this man and woman must die, must be cut off from Life," he continued, his resolve growing. "And their children and grandchildren -- everyone born from the dust of this world -- will forever be born into this death."

The Lord continued to instruct. "Creation is still governed by the Law of Love, the Law of Righteousness and the Law of Liberty. Every soul will be judged by those laws. The innocent, who walk this valley for only a few days, remain with Me. Those who choose to walk with Me are reserved. The rest will pass the same judgment as you."

The last phrase was the only part that made sense to satan, but he decided to press forward, probing his limits. "But what of those who choose neither Life nor death -- who live their lives indifferent to moral law? What will be their fate?"

"There is no neutral ground, no moral ambiguity. Eternity is set in every heart."

The Lord then concluded the discourse. "Because of what you have done this day, the curse that has fallen on this place has also fallen on you. This man and woman, made from dust, have given their authority to you and that is all you have. The dust of this earth is now your food and the place where you will dwell. That is the extent of what you have gained here today. You may attack their bodies and minds, but their souls remain free to choose between Life and death."

For the first time in many ages, the two foes looked intently into the other's eyes.

A similar scene would often be played on the earth. A scene where two brothers, two friends, two neighbors -- destined to oppose each other in battle -- would gaze for one last moment, remembering their love and friendship. In that moment, each would know that their next encounter would end in blood.

And so, with brief pause, God and Lucifer stopped and remembered.

Lucifer remembered the days near the throne when he would worship the Holy One; his heart and God's heart united. His own being was whole and filled with Glory. That single memory flickered for an instant and almost produced a spark. His features almost softened, his body almost relaxed and joy almost touched his heart. But then it was gone, shattered on the anvil of his bitter soul.

In that same moment, the Lord looked at His friend and remembered the bond they shared. He recalled the eons they had and how they had worked to oversee and bless creation. The Lord still loved him and would have offered him forgiveness, if He could. But those times were passed. The archangel of God, the one near the throne, had passed into death, destroyed in the emptiness of one who turned away.

"Your move," satan mocked, "but remember that the board is under my authority."

The devil's taunts only revealed his ignorance, for he did not realize that Redemption's course was already drawn and the first moves had already begun. The Lord knew what must be done and how the battle would unfold, but all must remain protected and allowed to proceed in its own way. In order for Redemption's work to succeed, the plan must stay hidden and the Redeemer's Song remain unsung -- for now.

2. Redemption's Plan

Then, the Lord began to grow in size, His countenance fierce. A quiet roar issued from His heart. It was then that Satan noticed something that he had not seen since the ancient battle, for the Lord had risen again as a Man Of War.

The edges of the Lord's countenance, the soft Light and Glory that rimmed His Person, became solid and took shape. The Lord's armor was revealed. With breastplate, helmet, shield, belt and shoes, the Warrior stood. The armor was of indescribable Glory --

fashioned from strands of Light that moved without the slightest hindrance or restraint. Each piece seamlessly joined with the other pieces to form a unified, impenetrable protection. Each subtle movement, each gesture from the Lord was perfectly matched. Each piece was alive, drawing substance from the One who wore it.

Within the armor, the Lord's mighty sword was revealed. The sword was fashioned from the strongest, most powerful material, yet it was also alive – sharper and stronger than anything in creation. It was immense and weighty, but light as air in the Warrior's hand.

Satan shuddered as he remembered the ancient battle when he was cast out. He remembered the shield that he could not penetrate and the sword that had no match.

Then the Lord began to rise from the earth. Taking the handle of His sword in both hands, high above His head, He thrust the tip into the dust and spoke Redemption into the earth. His voice thundered to the farthest reaches of all the realms,

"And I will put enmity between you and the woman, and between your seed and her seed. The seed of woman will crush your head, but you will bruise His heel."

With the same powerful Word that was used to create the worlds, the Lord had just planted the seed of redemption into the earth -- a Redeemer would come, a Savior, born of a woman, to release the captives, to conquer satan and to set the stage for sin's final judgment.

As the final echoes of the Lord's proclamation died out, the two faced each other one last time -- One filled with Love, the other with rage.

Then, a peaceful breeze stirred, and, for a moment, it seemed that even time had stopped. A brief, brief moment that was no longer than a sigh but that felt as large as eternity itself. That single moment that would be repeated many years later on a barren hill, with God hung on two pieces of wood. And in that future moment, the Lion of God, the Redeemer, would once again look into the face of His foe and, in that moment, declare "IT IS FINISHED."

The deceiver was perplexed. "What could this mean? How can there be a seed from the woman? How can God come into a world that has given its authority to me?" He wasn't sure, but He did know that the Lord never spoke empty words. So, even though he did not understand, he reasoned that his initial plan would still be the best course. He must resist all good, destroy all hope, and persecute everyone who tried to follow righteousness. Then, no matter how this "seed" arose or when it came, he would be ready.

So the battle began with simple phrase: "The seed of woman will come; you will bruise His heel, but He will crush your head."

With this, the Lord announced His opening move --
"the King's gambit," as it is called in the game of chess.
He would come to the earth, wrapped in lowly cloth.
As man, He would have the right to walk the planet
and to occupy a single place in space and time. And
there, like the lowly pawn, stand in the center of the
board and offer Himself as a sacrifice.

3. Death

From the shroud, from the mist, from the void, a new
enemy appears – Death
Ominous in power, unrelenting in its pursuit
Without real form, hideous in its lack of feature
With hollow face that showed no pity for elder or babe
Ravenous, feeding always -- never satisfied
At times in the shape of a man
But always an empty shell
A faint, red glow inside a thick black pall

The human race begins its descent
The downward pull is not resisted
The single path grants no parole
The tormentor awaits its prey

Darkness – the absence of Light
Death – the absence of Life

Chapter 4.
The Darkness Manifesto

The devil set to work his way
To lift himself, bring down the Lord
His hatred forged through many years
Secure and smug in plots and schemes.
O'r the years, as he would toil
He would be known by many names
Each name reflected his true self
Each an image of his soul:

> satan (adversary)
> devil (slanderer)
> abaddon (destruction)
> prince of darkness
> deceiver
> apollyon (destroyer)
> father of lies
> beelzebub (lord of the flies, lord of dung)
> accuser

His plan was simple in strategy and execution, and so he set to words the twisted designs of his wicked mind.

THE DARKNESS MANIFESTO

To all who follow me, attend and obey:

The authority of the earth is now mine, and we must fight to hold what has been gained. It is your job, it is our mission, to destroy, resist, persecute and pervert any attempt at good that might fester in this fallen race. Your job, put simply, is to press on human hearts, desires, minds and wills until they feel that my way is the only choice.

To accomplish this:

Pride. Pride is our primary tool, because it opens the door to destruction. The humans have chosen knowledge and independence over Life and Love, thinking to make themselves like gods. This is the element that supports our efforts. We must keep people's attention on themselves, their accomplishments, strength and intellect. By this constant focus, they will be convinced that they are improving and growing into a higher state. Each perceived advancement will be seen as the result of human effort and design. Each perceived failure will be seen as a lack of knowledge and a failure of plan. They will see no need for God, have no sense of their fallen state and have no perception of the shadow that shrouds their world. The sense of personal or group accomplishment or failure, without moral reformation, will make them willing subjects in my kingdom.

The Six Foundations:

Once pride is established, our efforts will rest on six foundations:

Destruction: Destruction follows pride. Now that humanity has turned from God, the blessings of Heaven cannot flow to the earth in the same way. The amount of effort required to merely survive is much greater than before, and the earth's environment has been compromised. We will use this to our advantage, because the universe that they know now tends toward chaos and destruction. The work of years and the toil of generations can be consumed in moments, rendering the efforts meaningless. The weapons for this are obvious and easy to use – war, disease, lawlessness, oppression, natural events and calamities. Combined with deception, we will convince the humans that the Lord or some higher force is actually releasing these destructive events. A single occurrence, a single person or a handful of well-placed followers can undo the sacrifice of generations. This downward slide of the physical world, the pull toward disorder brought by moral decay will give us an advantage. We will keep men and women focused on things of the earth and keep their hearts invested in temporary accomplishments that will only evaporate over time.

Distraction: With the constant cycle of building, destruction, and rebuilding, the earth dwellers will somehow convince themselves that any problem can be solved with human craft and effort. Each new group will see itself as better than the last and will believe that new methods will succeed where others have failed. But, each new house built on the sand of human wisdom will fall just like the one before it. This earthly focus and inward look will keep their thoughts away from God. Their brief earthly existences will consume their thoughts and keep them turned away from eternity. As a result, they will be convinced to spend the small time they have on earth in pursuit of little more than their own survival and happiness.

Desire: Personal wants and needs are central to keeping the heart turned inward and away from God. We remember that pleasure was actually created by the Lord and every soul is naturally drawn toward the pleasant aspects of true Life. Our task then becomes simple – take the natural desire to move toward Life's goodness and twist it.

The twist comes in two ways. First, inflame a subject's desires to pursue what is evil and forbidden – that is, tempt the subject to act contrary to God's Law Of Love. The second twist is more subtle. When basic human hopes and desires are crushed by the hardness of life, we will use disappointment to create anger and despair. We will then stir those emotions to create accusations and hardness against the Lord and each other. This will further separate the subject's heart from the Lord and drive them away from Love. In the end, unfulfilled desires will be even more effective than desires that are overtly sinful. It is a great victory when we convince the subject that life's hardships come from God.

Sin has brought destruction and heavy toil into the earth. People will long for rest and relief from our torment and will look to feed their souls on whatever they can find. We must convince them that pleasure, happiness, enjoyment and fulfillment can be attained apart from God, not through Him. They must believe that He wants them to be miserable and needy. Corrupted desires will make pleasure, rather than God, the goal of life. Fame, power, greed, lust, food, diversions – the list is endless – will all be served on my table, and, although these self-centered pursuits can never satisfy, it is the inner hunger of an empty soul that will make it hard for people to leave my table.

Division: It is important that, once we have isolated people into little groups, we constantly sow discord to keep them divided. For this, we use slander, gossip, faultfinding, suspicion and jealousy. Division among families is the most important, because once families are weakened, the rest becomes easy. We will build walls between groups, philosophies, races, cities, regions and nations. Wherever there is a difference, we will exploit it. Once the people are divided, we pick off the weak and mold various groups to be more easily controlled.

Deception: Eternity is set in every heart, so we must drown that voice in an endless chorus of deception. The people of the earth will constantly ask, "Who am I?" "Why am I here?" "Is there any purpose other than my own existence?" "Is there a God?" These questions will be a natural part of their earthly lives, but we must keep the questions buried. To do this, we will create whole systems of false religions, empty philosophies, human intellect and education that have no moral basis. We will feed their ego by providing arguments and systems built on the notion that their time on earth should be lived without God. In addition, we must keep them focused on an ever-changing stream of empty jargon, phrases and ideas. With this, they can be convinced of their own self-rightness, be manipulated with simple phrases and be kept busy accomplishing nothing of eternal value.

Domination: Replace God's law with the shifting morals of the crowd. Once Heaven's morals are rejected, right and wrong are little more than the exercise of earthly power and control. If people will not govern themselves by Love, they have given control over their lives to someone else. From this, we will herd the people into ever-changing groupings that espouse shifting and empty goals. We promise them liberty, but lead them into bondage. The so-called intellect of man can barely conceive of the true freedom that comes from moral choices, so they will always build systems where power is centralized and people are easily controlled. In that way, we need only control a few in order to control the masses.

The Six Strategies:

Pride: Always remember -- human pride is your ally.

Attack with the flies, conquer with the beast. To set up an attack, send in smaller demons first to probe for a weakness in character and soul. The smallest crack or compromise is enough. Once you find a weak spot, start to build a doorway so that larger, more powerful spirits may come through.

Use Your Weapons. Lies, torment, fear and pain are your weapons. Always attack. These humans are weak in their spirits, but proud in their minds. They are vulnerable. Find a weak spot and work from there.

Stay hidden. Never reveal yourself unless, in doing so, you can bring the subject into greater bondage. Most of the time, the subject must not realize the scope of your influence. Your greatest success occurs when the subject adopts a thought you have planted, without being aware of the source of the thought. The subject should adopt each idea as their own and believe each idea was freely conceived. At that point, their vanity will take over to nurture and protect those thoughts until the subject's nature has changed to be like us.

Create servants and slaves. Once the subject willingly accepts your ways as his or her own, you can influence that person to act for you. Sin brings the subject into bondage -- use this. Use the humans to attack each other and create bondage. Then, use our weapons to build fortresses in lives, families and groups.

Destroy all good. Don't lose sight of the primary mission, which is to destroy good on the earth and create a haven for evil that even God will not penetrate. All good must be resisted, twisted and destroyed. Anyone who dares turn to the Lord and convince others to do the same must be destroyed. We must strive to prevent Love from gaining an advantage in the earth.

Conclusion. Remember that this Lord Of The Universe is the One who cast us out. He must pay for that. He is no fool, and He has great power, but He is bound to the Law of Love. This makes Him weak, because, under that Law of Love, each being must be allowed to choose. God will not violate that law. In contrast, our weapons are strong enough to overcome a puny will, once that will has rejected a relationship with God. There is a single, narrow path that leads to God, and it will be against the nature of the fallen race to walk that path. We will create a thousand other paths, to divert each soul away from the one path that leads to Life.

The earth will be ours. The human race will be ours.

We will prevail.

We will have our revenge.

Chapter 5.
Justice and Mercy

A. Justice

There Justice stood with watchful eye
Strong, resolute of heart and mind
Not blind, as is so often shown
No cruelty toward this fallen race.
Without vindictiveness or spite
He knew his course must never turn
No compromise allowed in part
No turning from the way ahead.

With purest sense of sight and sound
To penetrate the blackest realm
For shadows give no hiding place
To 'scape from Justice' perfect gaze.

With purest sense of sight and sound
To hear each word of lips and heart
No pretense veiled, no motive false
Could hide itself from Justice' sight.
For every action and its fruit
Plus every deed and consequence
Are all laid open, all laid bare
To one who sees with Heaven's Light.

With purest sense of sight and sound
The deep-set fear of human soul --
That sense that Someone always saw
Eternity within the heart.
That Justice watched and knew each thought
And someday sin's wage must be paid
That Someone saw and Someone heard
And someday all would be revealed.

To bargain or to compromise
Could not be done or ever thought
The fate of evil had been sealed
And there it must remain in bonds --
No yin, no yang; no slow détente
No place where sin could be at rest
No shades of gray allowed to be
No mixture of the good and bad.

Sin must be banished, sealed below
And there it must remain always
A tiny prison, deep abyss
There built as sin's eternal home.
No quarter would be ever found
No sanctuary for the night
No secret place where it could hide
Throughout creation's vast expanse.

But Justice was not cold nor harsh
No vengeance held within his heart
Exceedingly precise his role
For there could be no compromise.
Half-measures would not be proposed
Negotiations never held.

For there would be a future day
When all accounts are settled out.
Then every act receive its due
The Judge of all, each life review.
The records kept, the balance struck
Transgression's wage still to be paid.

The scale in Justice' hand tipped hard
It rested fully to the left
And there it stayed each passing day
Each godless act just adding weight.

No sacrifice of fallen man
No deeds, no acts, no skill, no craft
Could move the scales a single bit.

No intellect or cunning speech
No field of thought or human strength
Could move the scales a single bit.

B. Mercy

And Mercy waited patiently
Throughout the years that coursed the earth
With purpose calm and peace of heart
She interceded for the race.

She knew the time would soon arrive
When all requirements were fulfilled
Then she would rise, as if from sleep
Although her passion did not rest.
Her limits coming not from God
But set by lust within the race.

For mercy must come from the heart
And when the heart is turned from Love
She quietly stands there to the side
And only answers when she's called.

But Mercy's heart was never vexed
Was never wearied by the wait --
She knew God's sacrificial Love
And watched Him work Redemption's plan
She knew that God would pay the price
And watched the depths of His resolve
She knew that Justice must be firm
And every part must come to pass
She knew Redemption's time would come
The fall of man a short-time state.

So Mercy waited for her time
And looked for those few godly souls --
To show some good, some caring acts
To operate in few, small ways
To wipe the brows weighed down with toil
To comfort lives as best she could.

So Mercy waited for her time
She waited for that blessed day
When full-worked plan lets fly the verse
Redeemer's Song could then be sung.

C. Justice And Mercy

Justice, Mercy side by side
Were not opposed or set apart
A single heart, a single whole
They stood with purpose unified.
Redemption was their common goal
The darkness must be overcome --
All sin must be entombed below
The sting of death must be annulled
Defeated, not to rise again
For there must be a final blow.

So there they stood, together worked
Until they would be joined as one
United pair, inside a babe
The seed of woman, robed in dust.
A tiny child, a Sacrifice
Redemption planted in the earth.
A tiny child, a Sacrifice
The One to crush the serpent's head.

PART 3.

THE REDEEMER

Chapter 6.
Jesus, The Christ

A. Into The Fallen Realm

The path set out before our time
Held quietly in the secret place
The Son would come to pay the price
To show the Father to the world.
To every woman, man and child
To each among the fallen souls
Redemption would be offered free
To every heart that turned to Love.

From Glory's realm, past where we see
Jesus, the Christ, the Son of God
This tiny babe, the Prince of Life
The Sacrifice, now one of us.

Our God With Us, Immanuel
Encased in flesh, in lowest form.
Born to a virgin, blessed of God
The seed of woman, as foretold.

A suit of dust became His robe
A sweaty brow, His kingly crown.
This tiny babe, Creator, God
Had laid aside His prior rank --
To walk this realm, to feel our pain
To see our lives through human eyes
To show the Father to the world
To look at death as born a slave.

The Mighty One, the Lord Of All
Now condescends to weakest mode
Creator God, begotten Son
Has stepped upon the world He made.
In lowly state, to pay the price
Not subjugate, or force His way --
This babe, this Lamb, this humble mode
The One Who made the stars to be
In meekest tone, in stable born
Was hidden well until His day.

His parents poor, of no acclaim
A righteous house, but without note
By worldly means, of no repute
To bring Him forth, they bore the shame.
Content to do the will of God
To pay the price, to bear the Son
Redemption safe within their care
Protected far from satan's view.

The Father's plan was hidden well
Its strength and power buried deep
Against the wisdom of the world
Against religion of the day.
Who would have known? Who would have seen?
For few had heard Redemption's Song --
Notes softly hummed by ancient ones
Who longed to see Messiah come.

So Mercy scanned the scene with joy
Her heart was full from years of wait
Her time to work would soon arrive
To lift ones from their fallen state.
There Mercy stood with swelling heart
Redeemer here, Incarnate God.

As Mercy, Justice both looked down
This Infant One that seemed so frail
This Innocence upon the straw
Would soon assault the gates of hell.
They both could see the road ahead
The heavy load, the rocky path
The painful door which He must pass
For this could be the only way.

So Mercy looked on Justice' face
The two now joined in mortal frame
In quietness, both had sensed the peace
The Champion at last on earth.

The voice of Justice hushed, but firm
To speak the terms that must be met.
"It's not enough that He is here
It's not enough to walk the earth.
All must be finished, all fulfilled
The price for sin be paid in full
And evil must be overcome
The sting of death destroyed at last."
"Will He finish? Will He accomplish?"

Mercy answered, "He will."

So in the still, the silent night
The scales of Justice start to groan
Begin to shift in tiny range
As Life was soon to be applied --
Against the weight of all our sin
The single payment soon be made
The Son of God in sacrifice
Sufficient to atone the race.

B. The Early Years

The Father watched His Son prepare
To walk the steep and rugged path.

Three years were all the Son would have --
Three years, no more, to finalize
Three years to work Redemption's plan
To satisfy the law's demands
Then give Himself in sacrifice.

Three years He had to set the stage
Three years to walk and heal and teach
Three years to train his followers
And lay foundation for His church.
This church would hold Redemption's Song
And take it to the farthest land
But first the meaning must be taught
The first disciples understand.

The devil's plot must also run
The devil's plot be fully played.
The Sinless One must be cast down
The Innocent be falsely judged
A Righteous Life sent to the tomb
And this by an unrighteous act.

The Father pondered how to train
His Son for such an epic task.
He was not sent away to school
To temple, to be trained a priest
But stayed at home to work His job
A carpenter, a laborer.
He learned life as a working man
His sweat to earn His daily bread
To serve in His community
A single, honest businessman.

And there He labored in His shop
The Warrior-King, but who would know?
God's ways are so far from our own
True wisdom chose the higher path --
To learn God's heart from honest toil
For others' needs, to use His skill
To give full value for His trade
To do this every working day.

The workbench in His humble shop
Became the school desk for His life
His Father taught Him through His work
Prepared Him for the road ahead.

And through the scriptures He would hear
And understand Redemption's Song
To learn His task within the scrolls
As faith was growing in His heart.
To know His purpose and the fall
To know His Father and the plan
The Father's business, His command
Obeying as the Son of Man.

And just like Adam, years before
When work was done and sun was low
As day would cool, the Father came
To walk beside the Son of Man.
To teach Him the eternal Truth
Instruct Him in the way ahead
Our God inside a human case
The Son of Man, grew strong with grace.

And so He grew, this Son of Man
With strength of spirit, iron of heart
In wisdom sharp, beyond His place
The Son of Man, grew strong with grace.

C. Three Years Of Ministry

The proper time, the wait well spent
Messiah, King was shown to men
The Word Made Flesh now walked our soil
Anointed One, Immanuel.
In flesh, like us, lived every day
Went by the name – the Son of Man.

He taught us well and set the course
Revealed the ways and power of God
That life is lived by sacrifice
And Love, the greatest of commands.

To us, He showed the path to God
And laid aside His kingly robes
He walked and preached among the poor
A humble soul, a common man.

He dared to touch and fellowship
With those the world would throw away
With those upon earth's rubbish heap
Tossed out, rejected and disdained --
Diseased were touched and health restored
The broken hearted given hope
The harlot lifted from her doom
The cheating tax man shown respect.

For those who thought themselves in health
The Great Physician did not seek
But those who felt their need each day
Saw Mercy's face shown to the meek.

To walk with Him meant sacrifice
No place or power or acclaim
To not look back or wish for more
Nor wait until some future day.

His followers would pay the cost
This such a tiny price to pay --
To live each day for Heaven's will
To lay all down for Heaven's call
To give up what you cannot keep
Invested in eternity.

And, in each day, serve with whole heart
And not search for the world's applause
Nor write their gains upon the sand
Content with Heaven's record book.
Full knowing that the true account
Would be revealed when days are through.

Of those who toiled and scratched for bread
This Man must be from God, they thought
For no one spoke the way He did
And no one shared their suffering.
Messiah? Here? How could this be?
Our leaders have rejected Him
And yet He does the works of God
With mercy, kindness and with power.

He does not rise to lofty words
That please the ear, but starve the soul
No studied rhetoric from Him
Just simple phrases, filled with truth.

He also lived the words He taught
A servant and a man of God
With steady hand to Heaven's work
And God confirmed with acts of power.

So as He worked and walked the earth
He would be known by many names
Each name reflected His true self
Each name a marker of the Christ.
From many names, here's but a few:

Jesus (God Is Salvation)
The Son of God
The Son of Man
Messiah (Anointed One)
Savior
Redeemer
Lamb of God
God With Us
The Word
Prince Of Peace
Light Of The World
The Way
The Truth
The Life

D. Opposition

Against the wisdom of the earth
Against the teaching of the day
This carpenter set out to build
God's will and work against the grain.

A thorn, a barb to those in charge
To those who rode the peoples' backs
He must be silenced, must be stopped
The matter must be solved with death.

So satan set to play his hand
To press his will on simple minds
His only purpose – to destroy
And so he set to kill the One.
With fleshly weapons from his bag
To stir the passions and the hate
Drive leaders mad with murder's rage
To turn against the Innocent.

But still, Redemption's work advanced
In spite of all that hell could do.
An end in sight that few could see
All roads were leading to His death.

Hell thought that death was battle's end
But Heaven's plan had larger scope
Death never has the winning move
And Life would conquer in the end.
Not a failure, not a loss
The death of Christ, a turning point
The rugged cross would form a key –
Unlock the pathway back to God
Unlock rebellious hearts to Love
Unlock the hidden gates of hell.

Chapter 7.
The Passion

A. The Night Before

1. The Last Supper

As Jesus knew the end was near
He drew aside His chosen twelve
A final meal, a chance to teach
A final rest with those He loved.
Here in the place, an upper room
He showed the servant's role once more
His call for those who walked His path
Was not to rule, but was to serve.

He taught them of the covenant
To be established by His death
His body broken, blood poured out
Would open up the way to God.

2. The Betrayer

Within this scene of love and rest
Sat one who's heart was turned away --
Who sought for many other things
Who looked to reap an earthly prize
Who shunned the cost, the public scorn
And hoped to take a grander role.
For as their King would come to power
This Judas would be lifted up.

For since this chosen band was called
These men from lowly walks of earth
The tempter sought to find a gate
A hidden place where he could work.
His power not enough to bring
Destruction down upon the One
But only by the hands of men
Could Innocence be wrapped in death.

So evil searched for any means
A way to stop this One from God
As he had done so oft' before
He had to kill this Man of God.

In Judas, satan found a breach
And pressed him hard the few years past
To stir his passions, earthly lusts
His discontent, desires for more.

See there above his swirling head
A sickly glow from tiny imps --
Sent from their master far below
To seal the act, to raise a fort
To fix betrayal in his heart.

3. *The First Move*

But Jesus knew the plot conceived
Within the mind of he who turned
He handed Judas one more bite
And with that piece, the mind was sealed.
The plan was fixed, the will secure
He would betray the Chosen One.

As in the garden long ago
A simple bite, that one event
Would set in motion many more
A major shift in Heaven's war.
So Jesus sent him from the room
"What you have planned, do quickly now."

On to the leaders of his day
In secret, Judas told his plan.

They all stood 'round with serpents' smiles
Embraced, as brother, their new friend.
Those men who once had mocked his course
Now nod approval for this man --
The one who would betray the Christ
And hope for profit where he could.

They brought him in for their designs
As scriptures had so long foretold
Beginning move in hidden scheme
To add betrayal to their plot.

This dirty deed, formed in the dark
The people could not know their part
They needed someone from outside
And here, the Lord's own follower.
Now they could stay in shadows hid
No one would know or dare suspect
What they had done, what they proposed
With whispers and with earthly guile.

These leaders of religion, hard
Who raised up by the hand of God
Exchanged what little light they had
For money, title and respect
For worldly gain and praise of men --
Stark contrast to the humble Christ.

They claimed to speak on God's behalf
And to be keepers of the Truth
They knew the words that God had said
But did not understand His ways.

But when God came to walk their soil
And stood before them face to face
The group conspired within the night
To put God to an earthly death.

Now in that plan, resolve was set
The purpose of the will was strong
And with betrayal on the board
The scheme, the place, the time all set.
Small garish imps, with work complete
Would step aside for stronger force.

Apollyon stretched forth his hand
Darkangel from the lowest pit
Poured out upon these willing hosts
A slimy filth of toxic bile --
That flowed like death, but burned with flame
To rouse the nerves, excite the mind
To clarify the course ahead
This Christ of God must suffer death.

B. The Garden

At that same time, the Lord withdrew
A quiet garden planted near
Time to prepare and fix resolve
To gird His heart for what must come.
A final preparation time
Establish Heaven's full intent
To lock His will and mind to task
The next step in Redemption's plan.

1. Sacrifice Begun

And as He prayed in agony
Blood from His brow, like tears of sweat
Forced out His skin by massive strain
Against the sin and what must come.
His blood, His human life first spilled
The sacrifice, in prayer, begun.

As those drops fell and kissed the soil
The earth cried out in agony.
Convulsing as her Master bled
Creator's blood spilled on her soil
This almost more than she could bear.

The earth then sighed, she also knew
The weight of sinful deeds she bore
The guiltless blood in rivers poured
Upon her crust, she had absorbed.
She knew full well and groaned within
'Til one day she might be set free
And be renewed from years of strain
To be a home for the Redeemed.

2. *Next Stage Resolved*

Enormous strain on Perfect Soul
To call it done, to end the toil --
To count the world unworthy, lost
Go back, reclaim His rightful place
Withdraw the ransom, leave unpaid
Reject this world of fallen souls
Their chosen master, their reward
The wage of sin, still theirs to pay.

A single word would be enough
To lift this burden, change the course --
Transport Himself to realms above
Exalted back to Heaven's throne
Above this swirl of evil hearts
Those burning with malevolence
Those hearts so bent with common hate
Could quickly be a distant blot.

Three times the Father heard His prayer
"Let this cup pass, if there's a way
If I must drink, then let it be
But most of all, I do Your will."

The Father's will, Redemption's plan
The Word Of God from ages past
Forged strong within the fires of Love
Was tempered in the Savior's heart.

So He arose to face the path
No doubt, no shadow in His soul --
Disdain for satan's meager scheme
The shame, the pain were not enough
To turn Him from Redemption's course.

This world could only touch His flesh
And that He offered willingly.
For as they beat and pierced His form
An earthly chalice would emerge --
To hold the sin, disease and shame
That bound the fallen race of man
Within His body all contained
All sin within the Son of Man.

His only dread, the deepest blow
For there would be a moment when
Our sin would rest within His frame
His Father then must turn away.
The agony to be apart
From Love and Life and unity --
So near the tortured edge of hell
To be alone for the first time
And cut off from the Trinity.

The Godhead had forever dwelled
Three Persons as a perfect One.

C. The Unseen

Outside the earthly noise of life
Beyond the place where eye can see
The Light, the darkness each stood firm
Each worked its plan to reach the end.

1. The Angels

Above the garden's agony
The angels bowed in silent grief
To watch the suffering Lamb of God --
The King they served for countless days
The One they loved without reserve
Who they had worshiped for all time.

Each one would gladly take His place
A thousand times and think it small
To stop the suffering of their Lord
Prevent a single drop of blood.

But there they stayed, obedient
Accepting the Eternal's will
Not fully knowing what they saw
Content to hold their place, as told.

Angelic grief rolled forth in waves
All kneeled in homage, folded wings --
To understand the price of sin
The debt of man that must be paid
The Love of God, in full, revealed.

In silent worship, holding place
Some steady gazed, some covered face
Their music quietly on the ground
There was no song, there was no sound.

Another band, a warrior caste
Kneeled at attention, senses sharp.
They waited for the smallest word
Their armor neatly to the side
There ready to be taken up
In skillful stroke, be fully armed.

A single word they waited for
To rush the earth and save the Son
And in one breath, they could deploy
Raise shield around their suffering Lord.
In instant, stand there by His side
Ten thousand warriors to command
Sufficient might within the least
To force an army to its knees.

But they too had a part to play
To be in ready and obey
And they, just like the Sacrifice
Maintained their power in its place.
They held their passion under guard
And rested in the will of God
By God's command, they held their ground
To watch Redemption's story play.

2. The Realm of Darkness

(a) The demon hoards

From far below the garden scene
And from the dust that robed the earth
The swirling hiss from twisted souls
Began to swell in angry chorus --
"We have Him now, this Holy One
A few more moments, He is ours
We'll drag Him down to our domain
His star will hang here upside down.
Beneath our feet He will abide
The power and the day is ours."

That jarring taunt from long-parched lips
Gave strength and purpose to the mass
For they had waited endless time
To have revenge, bring down the Lord.
Now it was here, the time to act
And they could soon release their filth
Upon these puny human souls
To have them do darkmaster's will.

The earthly mob was called to place.
They swirled and cried and pushed for death.
This horde of ants, with minds so small
More beast than man within their minds
So easily provoked and swayed
So easily controlled and bent.

Above and 'round this forming troupe
This band of men to soon take stage
A sickly, greenish glow was seen
As worker demons set to task.

The demons galloped, surged and lurched
In search of willing hearts to bend
They pressed upon each fallen soul
In search of vessels they could use.

Into each vessel found was poured
An energy of blackest force --
Inflame the passions, set the will
To mock, to jeer
To cry for death
To beat, to flog
Inflict the blow.

So hell explored each human soul
And looked to find an opening
For players in their final act
To be assembled, each with role
Assigned to them from deep below
To play their part, shout their consent.

(b) The darkangels

In the dusk of early morn
Before the sun rose up in light
Out from abyss, from deep below
Three spirits came to walk the earth --
To take control, direct the mob
To drive tormented souls to task
To keep their troops upon the path
To press their servants into line.

Apollyon first took his place
Destruction was his specialty
He would conduct the means of death
Of cruel torment and of pain.
The leaders who had earthly power
Would bow and follow his command.
The Romans with their artful means
Of causing slow and painful death.
The leaders of religion, skilled
Manipulating hearts and minds.
These leaders of the fallen race
Exalted ones, so they supposed
Would start the chant, the jarring cry
"Crucify!" "CRUCIFY!" the Lord.

Next to come from deep below
Deception rose up like a mist
Without real shape, a shifting fog
He whispers lies, then he is gone.
His group would mold the minds of men --
To give them purpose, help them know
To plant his aim within their hearts
To make them think his thoughts as theirs
To keep their minds away from Light
To blind them to reality.

And finally upon the earth
Desire rose up and spread its feast --
To keep the simple to the task
Inflame their passions, twist their hearts
To burn and yearn and cry for death
To drive them by their earthly lusts
To crave each part they were assigned.

So with the clamor and the cry
Against the One who did no wrong
The shouts of death were clearly heard
"Crucify!" the Spotless Lamb.
This cry rose up from fallen ones
Against their only hope for good.
This fallen race so quickly turned --
So easy to manipulate
Forced on, tormented, driven mad
And reason, goodness nowhere found.

(c) Satan

With all the pieces laid in place
Revenge would soon be realized
Against the Judge Who cast him out
And dropped him into the abyss.

Satan knew the day was his
A skillful play in cunning plan --
To use the Lord's created ones
Ignite their souls with murder's flame
This wicked deed would seal his rule
Creator's blood upon their hands.

"How sweet," he thought, with sneer and smile
"That God's creation holds the key.
God's weakness is His heart to save.
God's folly -- to become a man."

"It's perfect," satan danced with glee
The Lord's plan had a fatal flaw --
For once the Lord stepped on the earth
And wrapped Himself in mortal shell
The Lord of Life, Eternal One
Now subject to the chains of death.

3. *Unseen Light*

The Light pulsed as a beating heart
With each new beat, its brightness grew
As fervor grew, a battle cry
Redemption's work was near complete.
The Father's heart to save His own
Began to pound, with patient zeal --
With peaceful joy, with triumph near
The veil soon torn, the bars unlocked
Forgiveness' door soon opened wide.

As Light raced from the heart of God
Intense and pure, but still unseen
The edges of the dark were pressed
Pushed back and started to recede.
The devil in his frenzied rage
Did not take note of the advance
That Light was moving from all sides
And starting to construct a cage --
To take back the authority
That satan thought was always his
To force him to give up the keys
To doom him back into the pit.

D. The Lion's Heart

Jesus bound and led away
He, by His will, held pow'r in check
He understood the path He walked
He had to let the dark plan play.

But why not make an end of this --
The swirling madness of the mob?
And why not call the angels forth
To render aid and recompense?
More than enough, His power strong
To stop the mocking and the pain
Humiliation brought to end
All could be stopped by His command.

But for this road, a single end --
The price of sin be paid in blood
Events allowed to run their course
'Til all the parts would stand in place
Redemption's plan be fully done
Redemption's Song must be complete.

So He allowed the tragedy
To play along 'till all revealed
Unfolding from tormented minds
With all accomplished, all fulfilled.
The sin of all within His frame
The guilt upon the spotless Lamb
The wage of sin, His sacrifice.

So to the cross, He journeyed on
With peace of soul and Lion's heart
He must confront the evil one
And stand alone there, face to face --
The seed of woman lifted up
To crush the serpent's head.

E. Mock Justice

The Roman empire ruled with iron
With sword and fist, enforced their peace
So skillful in the task of war
Unyielding to their enemies.
Their punishment became an art
Efficient, cruel to foster fear
For few would dare disturb the peace
And suffer swift, indifferent wrath.

To earthly judgment He was dragged
To face the Roman governor.
God mocked and beaten, bruised and pierced
The soldiers used Him for their sport.
A crown of thorns upon His brow
Tormentor's lash upon His back.
From every wound and slicing cut
Life's blood dripped free upon the dust.

So He was tried, and He was judged
The ruler found no fault in Him
No reason why He should face death
No crime to fit such punishment.

But bowing to the surging mob
The whispers on the ruler's ear
With show, declared the Innocent
Be led away and crucified.

F. A Brief Reflection

Here we pause, time to reflect
The scenes that play upon the earth.
The Heart of God, the heart of men
In these events, the Truth is seen.

1. *The Love of God*

Redemption shows the heart of God
We see His nature manifest --
Eternal Love, His Sacrifice
In perfect fullness, no reserve
His endless power wrapped in Good
Benevolence in every act.

God came to save and reconcile
He did not come to recompense --
But to the fallen world of men
The ones who turned away from God
But to the race that cursed His name
The proud ones so depraved by sin
But to the race that ran headlong
Into the twilight of the pit
But to the race that with each day
Found more cruel ways to waste itself
The race that soon would kill His Son --
An offer of forgiveness brought.

2. *The Human Soul*

To understand in little part
The twisted ways of endless night
Measured here on human scale
The nature of the human heart.
So here we pause to see the men
Whose lives were vessels of the plot
In contrast to the Heart of Love
Who gave Himself in sacrifice.

(a) The Roman Governor

The governor, the Roman man
With power, pomp to make a show
Sat in the judgment seat to rule
And look down from above the throng.

In end, he mocks the rule of law
His words condemn the Innocent.
A tiny pressure from the mob
And pretense falls, with truth revealed --
That earthly justice bows its knee
Protection for the ones who rule
Expedience the one, true way
To force the masses to obey.

For if the people turn from God
Exalt their might or boast their mind
Without the moral law of God
Corrupted power takes control.

(b) The Priests

The priests did likewise show their heart
Religious power in their hand
Position, payment they enjoyed
Held sway upon their congregants.

With doctrine sound, they quote the Law
And use it full for earthly gain
The praise of men, respectful words
Controlling all in their domain.

They traded service of the Lord
To buy and sell the souls of men
To hide the path to Heaven's gate
And build an empire on the sand.

They boldly said "the Christ will come"
Assured upon the prophets' words
They spoke about His future reign
God's kingdom come into the world.
And they would rule there by His side
His underlords upon the earth
But little did they understand
Their knowledge twisted for their gain.

This carpenter, who loved the poor
Became a threat to all they held.

Now in the end, when God did come
Messiah, longed for all these years
The priests removed so far from Light
They could not see that God was there.
So in the end, when God did come –

They killed Him.

(c) The Betrayer

In Judas, we can see ourselves
So quickly turned for selfish gain
For Judas shows us who we are
Our story in a single act.

For three years, Judas walked with Love
Called as a friend, there by His side
He heard the words and saw the deeds
But in himself refused the Way.
So in the end, with heart revealed
He sold his Friend for profit small
He turned betrayal into gain
And cashed his soul for one small meal.

To try and salvage selfish ends
He feigned a friendship to draw near
Betrayed True Love with single kiss.

(d) The Mob

For three years Jesus walked their paths --
He taught them peace, the way to God
He healed their sick and deaf and lame
Brought sanity back to the mind
He gave them food when they had none
He blessed the poor and raised the dead
To beggars, He was their relief.

So when He came, that final week
They shouted praises to their King
But here they are a few days hence
Still shouting as the Lord passed by.
But now they cry out for His death
They mock and laugh against His pain.
And to the One who brought them good
They, with one voice, call for His end.

G. Crucified

1. The Cross

A single tree, arms always raised
Unto the Lord Who gave it breath
Dragged from the soil, its life now stopped
Was hacked and cut to make two beams.
Was quickly chopped and crudely shaped
And forced to play this role in death
Repulsed that it was made to be
The place of torment for the King.

The Carpenter nailed to a tree
Here lifted up, the Sacrifice
And with three spikes, hung on a cross
His blood ran down upon the dust.

The world of man, the realm of sin
Had finished all that they could do.
Their pow'r and tricks now fully spent
With vicious taunts, they cheer His death.
For they could only touch His flesh
Beyond that place, they had no say.

With satan's moves now fully played
The death card turned, no more at hand
The Father set with master's stroke
Completion for Redemption's plan.

2. Final Hours

The Son of God
The Son of Man
Hung bleeding, bruised
Against the sky

A fragile case, that for short while
Had held the Lord in human form.
That fragile case, now broken, crushed
Abused until it lost its hold
Eternal Life, once housed within
Would soon escape Its mortal form.

And there He hung 'tween dust and sky
The Holy One now made our sin
His battered flesh, His earthly life
A freely offered sacrifice.

To human eyes, the wounds were foul
With gashes deep and flowing red
And even those whose minds were hard
Were sick from the brutality.
His flesh was torn and hung by threads
'Til few could recognize the man.

3. *The Forgiveness Prayer*

A single phrase, the mercy prayer
Forgiveness for this world of slaves
To bring to naught the reign of sin
The next atoning piece was laid.

"Father forgive them"

An intercession made in full
Release was prayed for fallen world --
For everyone who turned away
For those who mocked and laughed and cursed
And those who never saw that day.
Love's Sacrifice advancing on
To reconcile this race to God.

And with these words, a single prayer
Soft, quiet notes began to rise
From dying lips, Redemption's Song
Was heard from the Redeemer King.

The Father heard, the prayer was marked
Redemption's cry rolled through the realms.

4. *Sin Poured Out*

So as the Son hung in the sky
The Father placed upon His Own
The sin from all of Adam's line
The curse, the death and all despair --
All poured into the Holy One
All poured out on the Sinless One.

Beyond the place where eye can see
And human feeling has its reach --
Inside the stripes upon His back
Inside the wounds upon His brow
Inside the piercings in His hands
Inside the nail holes in His feet --
A foaming blackness, putrid rage
    death
    disease
    depravity.

Those things that plagued us since the fall
And all that formed our anguished tears
The shroud that fell to block the Light
And keep us from the reign of Love
Took root inside the Blessed One
Became alive within His wounds.

The Perfect One was made our sin
The sin of all on Perfect Soul --
The horror of each violent act
Each evil deed, malevolence
Each tear, each cry, all human pain
The sum of darkness in our lives
Such rancid waste and gnawing death
Now rested in the Son of God.

5. Darkness

As sin was poured out on the Christ
The Father took the judgment seat
He broke the bond with His own Son
In judgment, turned His face away.
There hung the Son, first time alone
As judgment reached into His soul
This separation so much worse
Than all the pains imposed by men.

The Son of Man now touched the void
A separation never known
To feel the anguish, as a man
Without a sense of Love and Good.
To know the weight of all our sin
To draw each breath apart from Life.

There on the earth, a thick, black pall
Descended on the hill of death
First slowly, almost not perceived
As nightfall clothed the mid-day sky.
For as the sin of all the world
Poured out, in full, upon the One
The Source Of Light had turned away
And shadow fell upon the Son.

The absence of Light
Descended on Calvary --
The place of the skull.

Part 4.

Redemption Realized

Chapter 8.
It Is Finished

A. Wisdom Revealed

The stage was set, the board arranged
The players all attending there
With Heaven, hell, earth's family
All now convened in single spot.

A single place, a single time
Four thousand years had spanned the earth
Since God and satan stood opposed
And gazed on each for one last time.
In garden's soil, the battle drawn.

Since God announced Redemption's plan
Both Light and dark had worked their ways
Both working to this single point
Where Good and evil intersect.

For death was satan's final play
And all his work now drove to this
Eliminate the Chosen One
And hell would rule triumphantly.

The greater Wisdom, hidden well
In Innocence, the Sacrifice
That God Himself would pay the due
Lay down His life upon the earth.
The law of God to be fulfilled
The covenant sworn in His blood.

For all the knowledge from below
Mixed with the wisdom of the age
Had failed to grasp what sin had caused
Or understand the remedy.

B. The Final Move

Inside the wounds by cruelty laid
From deep inside that Perfect Soul
The sin of earth was lodged and wrapped
There to be paid and reconciled.

The Son rose up, this was His time
The Lamb of God, bowed down no more
For in His frame, within His heart
He firmly held the sin of all.
Demands for payment, all decrees
Laid on the table of His soul
Sin's wages due from all mankind
All claims could now be satisfied.

For he had quietly held His strength
Allowed events to run their course
Now, with strong grasp, He held it all
Contained within the Sacred Heart.

C. Finished

The Son held firm within His grip
The sin poured out upon His soul
And from the judgment, no escape
To dig or burrow or take hold.
And for the Lamb, hung on the tree
His countenance began to change
A holy fire, with strong resolve
Began to burn within His eyes.
Through wounded features on His frame
His armor now was manifest.

And satan starts to sense a dread.
His bag of weapons fully spent
His strategies now fully set
And yet the battle was not won.

This Lamb of God, once meek in death
Began His final move as man.
He would not let the devil flee
But held sin strong by Heaven's might
And bound it firm with unseen cords
Upon the altar until death.

Then,
A stillness fell, a quiet calm --
Like tide gone out, paused to return
Like breath drawn in, and all is stilled
Before the next word issues forth
Like single space, a brief repose
Before the next beat of the heart.

An eager hush, an infant peace
Here, in the midst of battle fierce
The Son of God then raised His head
The time was here, and He had won.
A tiny smile crossed lips near death
Redeemer's Song would soon be sung.

From vilest place a soul had known
Pushed through the shroud around His Soul
From wounded flesh that gasped for life
The deep abyss of One made sin.
From final breaths of earthly air
The voice of Love was strong and clear,
Out from the gentle Lamb of God
The Lion roared, and all could hear,

"IT IS FINISHED."

D. The Chains Of Death

And so the Prince, the Lord Of Life
Suspended low above the earth
With arms outstretched, with body pierced
Flesh bruised and torn, 'til life was gone.

The heart of God, in human shell
This heart now broken from the load
The earthly sacrifice complete
The Christ let go His human form.

The chains of death rose from below
Death swirled to claim another soul
The Holy One would soon be dragged
Pulled down as death's new prisoner.
Entombed in darkness for all time
The Holy One there on display
A trophy for the lord of dark
A witness to the reign of hate.

The mist of death rose round the corpse
To wrap the Soul from body freed
The mist of death, the master cruel
That drove men to a common dread.
So many times, through ages past
This scene was played as breath was lost
So many times, without a fail
Each soul was dragged into the night.

And here the Prince was easy prey
So vile with filth from all mankind
So bathed in sin, so stained was He
Here no escape, parole could be.

Death's ending blow had landed cruel
Just like on countless lives before --
It never failed to reach its mark
It never failed to snag its prey
It never failed to bind a soul.

How could this be? Chains could not bind!
They missed the mark for the first time.
This Soul could not be captured, bound
How could this One resist the pull?
All prisoners had meekly come
To march to death's relentless drum.

Chapter 9.
Victory

A. Darkness Conquered

But still He came, the Unbound Soul
By His own will walked the abyss.
He was not forced or pulled or drawn
This Prince of Peace, this Man of War.

He did not go there bound in chains
But clothed in armor formed from Light
Unhindered march to satan's lair
The Champion invades the night.

As He approached the gates of hell
The bars flung open, off their hinge.
Without defense, no hiding place
What could protect the lords of dark?
The Victor clothed in Heaven's might
The Lion roared and stalked His foe --
The Son of Man, the Sacrifice
The Son of God victorious.
The Warrior King was in their realm
All they could do was hide and wait.

As He drew near, the darkness waned
The Son arose with Endless Life.
And in that Life, a Light was shown --
A Light not seen within this realm
A Light that pierced the thickest veil
That left no crack or hiding place.

He set His path straight to the core
The place where satan had his throne.
A feeble chair, built up on sand
And here darkangels tried to hide
Their voices loud with bickering
And passing blame, at war within.

Death, the fool, had let Life in
And with that slip sealed death's demise
For Light and Love had pierced the dark
The pit that demons called their home.

The Holy One now faced His foe
Just like the battle long ago --
But here no struggle, fight, no toil
For death succumbed, without a blow.
With perfect justice, all fulfilled
Death lay submissive before Life.

Low satan bowed, face in the sand
The weight of Glory pressed him down.
For every knee will humbly bow
Before the Lord Victorious.
The Lamb of God, with Lion's paw
Had placed His foot on satan's neck
And there fulfilled the prophecy
Proclaimed in garden, long ago.

The Lord reached down and took the keys
Reclaimed from satan's trembling hand
Authority in every realm
Now rested in the Son of Man.

Hell's plans and schemes, its thirst for blood
Had failed again and sealed their fate
So sure they were that they had won
Secure that power flowed from hate.
But, once again, they grasped a lie
Their knowledge being soiled by pride
Again they failed to overcome
Again rebellion came to naught.

With eyes that glowed blue from the flame
That rose inside the Victor's heart
The Lord Of All gazed on His foes
And left no doubt Love conquers all.
They cowered, ran, sought place to hide
But Jesus' eyes saw everything.

None dared protest or raise a hand
But only begged that He would leave --
Just leave them in their misery
Just leave them in their dark estate.
For, to them, this Holy Fire
Had caused more dread than all the night.

So there He stood, the Lord Of All
Victorious in every part
Redemption's Song could now be sung
Sung here within the darkest place.
Eternal good news filled the air
The captives heard and hope was born.

Oh death where is your piercing blow?
Oh grave, what victory is yours?

Some righteous souls, there bound in chain
Beheld the Dawn and hurried near
These souls had seen with eye of faith
And waited for this day to come.
For those whose lives had been prepared
And trusted God within their hearts
Heard the song Redemption sang
And followed quickly to the Light.

Then Sunday came, and He was gone
The gnawing black of night returned.
For demons, a new sense of loss
Tormenting pain, with something more
The pain of knowing they had failed
And soon would face the judgment day.

B. Resurrection

1. The Guarded Tomb

The body of the Christ lay still
Enclosed inside an earthly cave
Entombed in rock, in earthly sleep
A massive stone placed on the grave.

Outside the tomb, the stone was sealed
With Roman crest, a warning clear
That none should interfere or pass
And risk the wrath of Roman law.
Outside the tomb, the soldiers stood
They kept a watch to guard the dead.

So skilled and hardened for their job
No earthly force could pass their shield
These soldiers knew that if they failed
That they would pay with their own lives.

2. Resurrected

The Son of Man went back to earth
Stood by His body in the tomb
Two angels there at head and foot
Stood watch as o'er the mercy seat.
This robe of dust, now three days cold
Preserved until the Lord's return
Laid down in death, placed in the grave
'Til He would come and resurrect.

"Oh death, where is your victory?
Oh grave, where is your painful sting?"
Heaven's Warrior gently sang
As He retrieved His earthly shell.

With single word from Endless Life
His body was revived, made new
Without corruption, free from death
Recast from substance not of earth.

His body glorified, restored
In quietness lay upon the stone
With earthly scars still visible
Reminders of Redemption's cost.

The wounds that once held all our sin
Those wounds were cleansed and were transformed.
The scars were healed and Glory shown
Inside the place of sin's cruel sport.
For Love had conquered death and hate
The ugly scars now beautiful.

Eternal Spirit, Breath of God
Breathed gently on the silent case
The Christ reclaimed His human form
Rose up and left the stony slab.
And there He stood upon the earth
But now with body glorified.

As Glory surged in every cell
And washed o'er every nerve and bone
The Son arose, alive again
And Glory thundered from the throne.

The angels all, with single voice
Began to shout the great hallel
A mighty chorus unified
That rumbled through eternal realms --

"For the Lord God omnipotent reigneth
And He shall reign forever and ever
Hallelujah, Hallelujah."

And as the angel voices swelled
The universe began to sing
The stars in far-off galaxies
Lift up their voice in mighty shout.
A multitude, who with one voice
Like roaring ocean, thundered praise
A massive worship rolling forth
And all creation joined the song --

"Hallelujah
For the Lord Our God the Almighty reigns."

3. *The Grave Could Not Hold*

Outside the quietness of the tomb
The earth joined in Creation's praise
The earth began to rumble, shake
As she began her dance of joy --
Her Master's feet upon her soil
The curse of sin at last removed.

The tomb itself did also quake
With all its might to grip the bars
A final struggle to prevail
To keep the Lord inside its gates.
A feeble try to keep back Life
But Life was more than it could hold --
Such power could not be contained
And so the grave was overcome
And, in the end, it stood aside
And bowed submissive to the Lord.

4. *He's Alive*

A mighty angel then appeared
And joined the praise from all the realms
He landed on the massive stone
And rolled it back with joyful dance.
The angel's robe flashed forth with Light
And Glory showed from every strand
With beams of splendor, shining forth
As lightning from the noon-day sky.

The hardened soldiers shook with fright
The scene too much to comprehend
Their callous strength gave way to dread
They fainted, dropped, just like the dead.

Out from the tomb the Master walked
The Force of Life victorious
No chains could bind, no force could hold
This Undisputed Conqueror.
The keys of death and hell now His
Authority now in His hand
Triumphant to the last degree
His foes a stool beneath His feet.

5. *The Mercy Seat*

One final act, His to complete
Redemption's work had one more part
Ascended back to Heaven's home
His blood upon the mercy seat.

Chapter 10.
Redemption Complete

"It's Finished!" Justice bowed His head
His heart was quiet that all was done
The gavel firm had landed hard
But landed on the hand of God.

"It's Finished!" Mercy rushed with joy
Her intercession now complete
She leaned aside to her old friend
And placed a kiss on Justice' cheek.

When I survey the wondrous cross
On which the Prince of glory died
My richest gain I count but loss
And pour contempt on all my pride.

Forbid it, Lord, that I should boast
Save in the death of Christ my God!
All the vain things that charm me most
I sacrifice them to His blood.

See from His head, His hands, His feet
Sorrow and love flow mingled down!
Did e'er such love and sorrow meet
Or thorns compose so rich a crown?

Were the whole realm of nature mine
That were an offering far too small;
Love so amazing, so divine
Demands my soul, my life, my all

When I Survey The Wondrous Cross
Isaac Watts (1707),

Epilogue

Back on the earth, for forty days
He walked among the faithful ones
Revealed Himself, revealed the Word
And sealed in them Redemption's song.

For forty days, His followers
Commissioned in the task ahead
Sent forth to go throughout the lands
To teach the world Redeemer's Song.
Now sent into the fallen realm
Ambassadors for Heaven's King --
To live their days on bended knee
To reconcile men back to God.
Our King has offered pardon full
Redemption's price was freely paid
The church was given the good news
To carry hope to those in need.

Forgiven now, this race could be
For those who would repent, believe
The righteous nature of the One
Imparted to believing souls.
The covenant, the law of God
Could now be written in the heart --
Not carved in stone or taught from books
Not practiced in repeating rote.

The lives of all could now be changed
Transformed, made new, and turned to God
To grow in likeness to the Lord
And walk the footsteps of the Son.

Again, God's wisdom hidden well
Revealed to those who would obey
The simple word, two letters long
Is God's command --"go" to the world.

Devotion simple, faith unfeigned
Our worship strong from thankful souls
With honest lips and open hands
Our lives laid down upon the cross.
To love the Lord with all our heart
To love our neighbors as ourselves
To reach the poor and those without
Those tossed aside by worldly ways
To clothe and feed, to offer hope
To visit those in need, in jail
For here we find our Lord at work
And here we touch the face of God.

An Invitation

Who knew? Who even dared to dream that this God of infinite power is also Love Itself? God, who wears the stars of a billion galaxies like a robe, has created us to have a relationship with Him and to be part of His family.

But we chose independence over this Life. By our actions individually, and in groups, we daily tell the Lord that we choose to live without Him, that we prefer to live life on our own. So, He waits patiently with the front door always open, waiting for us to return, waiting for relationship, waiting to show His Love.

When Jesus was on the earth, he told this story:

A certain man had two sons: And the younger of them said to his father, Father, give me the portion of goods that falleth to me. And he divided unto them his living. And not many days after the younger son gathered all together, and took his journey into a far country, and there wasted his substance with riotous living. And when he had spent all, there arose a mighty famine in that land; and he began to be in want. And he went and joined himself to a citizen of that country; and he sent him into his fields to feed swine. And he would fain have filled his belly with the husks that the swine did eat: and no man gave unto him. And when he came to himself, he said, How many hired servants of my father's have bread enough and to spare, and I perish with hunger! I will arise and go to my father, and will say unto him, Father, I have sinned against heaven, and before thee, And am no more worthy to be called thy son: make me as one of thy hired servants. And he arose, and came to his father. But when he was yet a great way off, his father saw him, and had compassion, and ran, and fell on his neck, and kissed him. And the son said unto him, Father, I have sinned against heaven, and in thy sight, and am no more worthy to be called thy son. But the father said to his servants, Bring forth the best robe, and put it on him; and put a ring on his hand, and shoes on his feet. And bring hither the fatted calf, and kill it; and let us eat, and be merry. For this my son was dead, and is alive again; he was lost, and is found. And they began to be merry. [Luke 15:11-24 KJV]

God has opened a way so that everyone has the chance to return to Him. That is the purpose of Redemption; that is the Redeemer's Song. In that one act, God became our substitute and took the penalty for our rebellion on Himself. In Redemption, we see the perfect harmony between Justice and Mercy, between Holiness and Love.

And just like our early parents in the garden so long ago, each of us has a choice to make – do we accept a life based on Love or do we reject that Love in favor of a life of seeming independence? God has done everything that He can to restore this relationship, but He will not force anyone into it. Love will never force or manipulate, but always allows for a choice.

If you have never given your life to God and trusted in the work of redemption, God invites you to come home today.

So how do you do this?

There are no magic words or formulas. Just be honest, because God will always hear the prayer of an honest heart. Don't try to impress God or fool Him with fancy words. He already knows everything. Be sincere.

When Jesus was crucified, two criminals were also crucified at the same time. One of the men was shouting insults at Jesus.

> *But the other answering rebuked him, saying, Dost not thou fear God, seeing thou art in the same condemnation? And we indeed justly; for we receive the due reward of our deeds: but this man hath done nothing amiss. And he said unto Jesus, Lord, remember me when thou comest into thy kingdom. And Jesus said unto him, Verily I say unto thee, To day shalt thou be with me in paradise. [Luke 23:40-43 KJV]*

Here we see that, from one simple prayer, a criminal in the middle of his own execution, found redemption. Apparently, he was not a religious man or one who had lived a "good" life. Still, the simple cry of his heart was enough.

If it helps, you could use the following prayer as a guide:

> *God, I realize that I have tried to live life without You and that I have sinned. I am sorry for my sins. Please forgive me. I trust in the death and life of Jesus and place my faith in the work of redemption. I ask You to*

receive me and make me part of Your family. Thank You for accepting me; thank You for eternal Life.

Even if you are not ready to come home right now, then tell God and ask Him to speak to you and to show you His truth and perspective. He will speak to you when you are ready to hear.

Here are a few closing thoughts that might help:

<u>Salvation (where God forgives us and brings us into His family) is an act of faith.</u> We can never do enough good to earn it or do enough bad so that we do not qualify. The Bible says, *"That in the ages to come he might shew the exceeding riches of his grace in his kindness toward us through Christ Jesus. For by grace are ye saved through faith; and that not of yourselves: it is the gift of God. Not of works, lest any man should boast."* [Ephesians 2: 7-9 KJV].

<u>There really is a God, and He is good.</u> God is not a religion or an idea. He really does exist on His own and apart from our ideas about Him. He is eternal. He is infinite in Love, Holiness and Power. Although He is all-powerful, we do not serve Him or worship Him because of His power. We come to Him and worship Him because of His goodness.

<u>God will speak to an honest heart.</u> If you don't know, tell Him. If you're angry, tell Him. If you're wounded, tell Him. Then listen and trust Him speak to you at the right time. God is big enough and smart enough and loves you enough to talk to you. It is

important to keep the lines of communication open between you and God.

<u>You will live forever</u>. The only question is, "Where?" We all walk this earth for a very short time, but the real part of us -- the inside part -- will live forever. Those who have trusted in the work of Redemption will live with God. Those who have rejected God's offer have chosen to reside forever in the eternal prison that is reserved for those who rebelled.

<u>Eternity is forever; choose wisely</u>. Take a single grain of sand off the earth and launch it into the sun. Then, after a thousand years, do the same with a second grain of sand and continued to do this once every thousand years. By the time every grain of sand has been removed from the earth, eternity will still be going on. The real you, the eternal part, is of great value (valuable enough for the sacrifice of redemption). The choice of what you do with that eternity is given to you.

<u>Today is always the best day to come home to God</u>. Even though we will all live forever, our time on earth is short. We have no guarantees in tomorrow.

A closing prayer, for all of us.

That Christ may dwell in your hearts by faith; that ye, being rooted and grounded in love, May be able to comprehend with all saints what is the breadth, and length, and depth, and height; And to know the love of Christ, which passeth knowledge, that ye might be filled with all the fulness of God. [Ephesians 3: 17-19 KJV].

Additional Material

A. Table Of Contents

B. Artistic Credits

The following artistic properties are in the public domain or used by license:

1. Typefaces (licensed under the SIL Open Font License, Version 1.1, http://scripts.sil.org/OFL).
   a. Gentium Book Basic, by Victor Gaultney
   b. CINZEL, BY NATANAEL GAMA
   c. PT Sans, by ParaType
   d. PT Serif Caption, by ParaType
   e. Eagle Lake, by Astigmatic
2. The King James Version of the Bible is in the public domain in most of the world.
3. The artwork used on the cover and in the book is from an original work, in charcoal, by the author's spouse and is an adaptation of a pre-restoration portion of the Sistine Chapel ceiling, painted by Michelangelo between 1508 and 1512.

C. About The Author

The author is no one of importance -- just a person who deserved judgment and is extremely grateful for redemption.

D. Publisher Resources

Website:

http://www.mercy-media.com

Facebook:

https://www.facebook.com/redeemerssong

www.ingramcontent.com/pod-product-compliance
Lightning Source LLC
Chambersburg PA
CBHW071319130626
46556CB00004B/1662